Stories of

A Fall at the Quarry

Adv   an

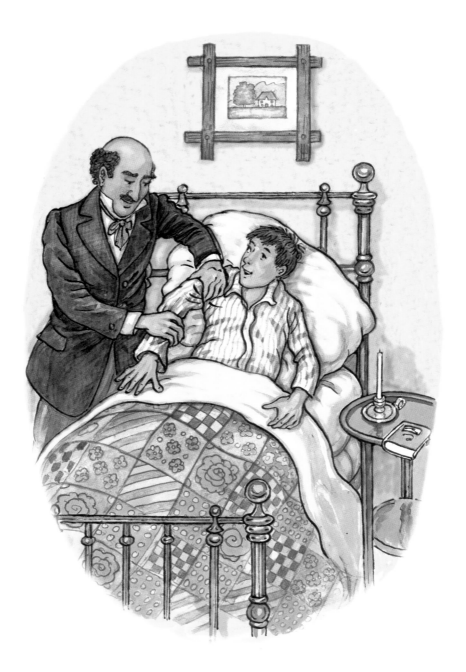

The doctor bent over me.

"Sparrowhawk," I said, talking fast to hide the fact I was scared. "It's a good name for a wild-car. A sparrowhawk swoops through the air like a flash of lightning."

The doctor laughed, as he examined my shoulder.

"I'm sure it does," he said. "Now calm down."

But I ignored him and carried on talking faster than ever.

I'm Jack Edwards, I said. I'm thirteen and I work in Graig Ddu quarry. Graig Ddu is on top of a mountain with rail tracks leading up to it. In the mornings us quarrymen climb into a wagon and get winched up the incline, but in the evenings we have to make our own way down.

Bet you've never tried trudging down a mountain at the end of the day when every part of you is tired and aching, Doctor, I said. It's hard work! I'm a rubbler, see. A rubbler is a boy who shifts rubble out of the way. In our quarry we make slates. To make slates, you first of all have to have stones, and to get stones, you blow up the mountainside with powder.

Boom! The rock face cracks and down come the stones. The big stones are used for slates, but there are plenty of little chips and splinters that are no good for anything. They're the rubble. Everywhere you look there are massive heaps of rubble. So no wonder I'm tired by the end of the day. That's why I need a wild-car.

With a wild-car you can get down the hill in eight minutes flat - or faster still, as long as you're careful not to tip over and break your bones.

A wild-car is simple, see, but brilliant. It's an iron bar with a raised edge called a flange at one end, and a wheel and a wooden board at the other. The flange and the wheel fit onto the two rails in the centre of the tracks. You sit on the board and – whoosh! - off you go flying down the mountain.

Most of the quarrymen I know have got wild-cars. Lloyd the blacksmith will make you one for five shillings, but I hardly earn that much in a month. It's true! Last Saturday pay day, for instance, I only had five shillings and two pence in my pocket to show for a month's hard work. Well, a month bar a day.

Let me tell you what happened to that missing day. A week last Monday it was. Five o'clock in the morning and Mam was shaking me awake. The stars had hardly faded against our frosted window, so I groaned and turned over. Ten seconds later I was out of that bed in a flash. It was Mam! She'd turned awkwardly and fallen. The clatter woke my sister Mary. Together we got Mam onto the edge of the bed, where she clutched at her right knee. In the twilight her face was as pale as the moon and the noise she made as she gritted her teeth sounded as loud in my mind as our gouger in the quarry. I held her steady, while Mary rushed to get a wet cloth.

For a while time stopped, and when it got going again and Mam was back on her feet, I was late. I left the house without my tea bottle, with hardly a bite of food in my stomach and only a torn-off hunk of bread in my food tin. The other men had long gone, leaving a muddle of black footprints on the white hoarfrost. I raced along the path puffing like an engine. If you turn up late at the quarry, George Watson, the steward, can send you home straight off and you'll lose a day's work. So there I was thundering along, when who should I see hurrying out onto the path in front of me, but George Watson himself. He was late too! What a stroke of luck.

"Good morning, Mr Watson," I called respectfully.

The steward looked over his shoulder and managed one of his clenched-teeth smiles.

"Good morning indeed, Jack Edwards," he replied.

"It wasn't so good for my mother, mind," I said, and, falling in beside him, I told him about Mam and how she'd slipped.

I think he understood me, though we don't speak the same language, for he shook his head in a sympathetic enough manner. Then we both climbed into a wagon and fell into a silence as we were hauled up the mountain. It wasn't till we got to the top that Mr Watson spoke again. As I stepped out of the wagon, flexing my shoulders and looking round for members of my crew, the steward said in his low growl, "You're late for work, lad."

"Yes, sir," I said.

"So you know the penalty for that."

"Sir?" For a moment I thought old George had a streak of humour after all, and he was teasing me good-naturedly as the regular quarrymen do. But when he turned to me, his face had no trace of a smile.

"Home, lad," he said. "No work for you today. You've turned up late at the quarry. Rules are rules." And off he went, leaving me to trek back down the hill and walk the four miles home, without the chance of earning a penny. Now what do you think of that?

What do you think of that mean-minded stickler for rules? He couldn't tell me to go home, when I first met him. Oh no. He had to wait till I got to my place of work before sending me off. George Watson didn't punish himself for being late either. It's one rule for him and another for us quarrymen, though we're the ones who do the work. We're the ones who keep the quarry owners in their fine mansions, yet we're the ones who suffer for it.

I expect you think I told him that to his jowly face. Well, I didn't. He'd have liked that, so I wasn't going to give him the satisfaction. I just gritted my teeth as hard as my poor mother had gritted hers that morning, and walked away at a steady pace with my head held high. As soon as I was out of his sight, I went running, mind. I started racing the slate wagons that were clanking down the incline. Our slates go to all parts of the world, you know. High quality, they are. They keep everyone snug and dry. Everyone except the quarrymen, that is, but I'll tell you about that later.

At that moment my anger was boiling up like water in a kettle. It drove me on down the path, faster than was sensible. Soon my legs were spinning so hard I couldn't stop them. Down I went flat on my face and rolled over and over down the hill.

I ended up with my elbow in a heap of rubble and my eyes shut against the morning sun.

"Ouch!" I said to myself. "Ouch! Ouch! Ouch!"

As I painfully heaved myself up, bits of rubble slithered and clattered down the path. That's when I saw this thing poking up out of the ground where that rubble had been.

That stopped my groaning. The thing, still half-buried in rubble, was a rusty iron bar. But not an ordinary iron bar. It was a bar with a flange at the end of it.

It was the underneath of a wild-car!

I didn't stop to think how that wild-car had ended up at the side of the track. I just grabbed hold of the flange, and tugged and pulled.

When the bar came out of the ground, all the anger left me. I whooped out loud and set off for home with a grin the size of a bargain on my face.

I scared Mam. Mam was standing at our door with the sack already round her shoulders. Despite the pain in her knee, she was about to set off to clean for Mrs Davies, Fronwen, as usual. But the sight of me running along with an iron bar in my fist drove all thoughts of pain from her mind.

"Jack!" she said in a faint voice.

My sister Mary appeared.

"Jack!" she shrilled, her eyes as frightened as Mam's. "What are you doing here now?"

"It's all right," I said, running up to them. But they shrank away, as if they'd seen a ghost, which they had in a way.

I'm like my dad, see. Same browny-black hair. Same bright blue eyes. Same long, lean face and beaky nose. Same hot-headedness. That's what scares Mam.

My dad was Dai Joss — David Joshua Edwards — though he was nicknamed the 'Sparrow'. Some of the men who work at the quarry are known as 'jackdaw boys', because they're the ones who have the worst pickings. But Dad was only called 'Sparrow' because of the nose, and because he was bright and busy too. He used to work at Braich quarry.

Remember what I told you about our slates keeping everyone snug but the workers? Well, that was definitely true of Braich quarry. Seven years ago the men at Braich had nowhere to shelter. As well as having to work in all weathers, they had to eat their midday crust outside as well. So what did they do? They built themselves a little cabin in their own time, where they could eat their midday meal away from the cold and the wind and the rain.

You'd have thought the management would approve, wouldn't you? Not a bit of it! That snooty lot didn't want their workers to be snug and dry. They claimed they had to lay a rail track in that very spot where the cabin was standing, and knocked it down. My dad was so angry at the unfairness of it, he picked up an iron bar and beat it against

the rails till the rocks rang with the sound. Dad was sent home that day, and not long afterwards he caught pneumonia and died. Mam thinks it was because he was too angry and hot-headed. She thinks his hot-headedness weakened him.

I don't think so. Do you?

Anyway when my mother and sister saw me running along with an iron bar in my hand and a mad grin on my face, they thought the worst.

"It's all right," I called. "I haven't done anything wrong. Well, apart from being late," and I told them how unfair it was that George Watson had sent me home. Then I said, "Look, I found a wild-car on the way down."

"A wild-car?" said my sister, forgetting her scare. (Mary would love to ride a wild-car.) "But that's not a wild-car!"

"It just needs a bit of board for a seat," I said.

"There's a broken bit of desk in the corner of our schoolroom," cried Mary. "Mr Davies was going to burn it on the fire, but…" She grinned at me. On account of being a bit of a scholar, I'd always been a favourite of Mr Davies's.

So that's how I ended up going down to the village with Mam and Mary that morning, and I was glad I did, because Mam could lean on me and take some of the strain off her sore knee. I was glad to get the piece of school desk too. It was solid and just right for a wild-car. I spent the rest of the day burning the rust off the iron bar, straightening a

bend in it and cleaning and rubbing and greasing.

I called it the Sparrowhawk after my dad, and carved the name on the underneath of the seat, along with my own initials. All the men carve their initials on their wild-cars.

I'd told Tom Jenkins about the Sparrowhawk straight off, so he wouldn't get jealous. Tom's my friend and he works with his dad on the same bargain as Sam Morris, the man I work for. D'you know what a bargain is? It's a stretch of rock face. You can't just go to a quarry and start chipping at any rock you like. A team of men have got to get together to bargain for it first.

When that's done, the rockman blows up the rock face. The large stones that fall down are cut into smaller sizes and shared out between the team members, who then split and cut them into slates. I'm learning to split and cut. Sam Morris gives me some of his stones to practise on, and I'm getting quite handy with the hammer and chisel. Not as handy as Tom, though. Tom works with his dad, who gives him lots of stone. That means he earns a lot more money than I do, because he makes more slates and you get paid for them at the end of the month.

So Tom wasn't jealous. But he warned me. This was on the Tuesday, the day after I'd been sent home.

"Don't bring the Sparrowhawk in just yet," he said, "because Watson'll be on the look out for you."

He was right. Wherever I went that day, I could feel the steward's eyes on me and his stocky dark shadow

hanging over me. It was as if he expected me to be angry and hot-headed, and was looking for an excuse to send me home again. In that mood, if he saw me with the Sparrowhawk, he'd want to know where I got it from, and maybe even claim I had no rights to it.

So I bided my time, and Mary and I spent so many evenings polishing and rubbing that wild-car, Mam said she would be quite sorry to see it go. She said it sparkled like a fancy ornament in our cottage.

Then this morning, bright and early – it was this morning, wasn't it? - I set out from our house with the Sparrowhawk on my shoulder.

Tom had promised to wait for me and we walked along side by side, with the Sparrowhawk between us, keeping a weather eye out for George Watson.

We were so early that it was only David Rees and Ianto Parry, two of the Anglesey men, who joined us in the wagon, all bleary-eyed. The sight of my wild-car soon woke them up, though.

"Hey," said Ianto, drawing his fingers down the polished seat. "Where did you get this, man? Only a quarry owner would have a wild-car as fine as this."

I laughed at the thought of a quarry owner sitting on a wild-car instead of riding in a fine carriage.

"I made it," I said. "From scrap."

"Where's the brake then?" asked David.

"There isn't one," I said. "You don't have to have a brake."

"We'll have to get out of your way tonight then."

"Yes." I sucked in my breath, looked down the icy tracks and wished I could go flying down them that moment. But I couldn't. I had eleven long hours to wait.

When we neared the top, I could see the heap of wild-cars. After the men have reached the bottom of the incline, they throw their wild-cars into a wagon, which gets pulled back up ready for the next day. All the cars looked dull and dusty. Mine looked like a jewel amongst them, so I hid it underneath in case someone fancied a go on it. Or in case Mr Watson noticed it, which would be worse still.

It was a cold old morning, with the sun like a sheet of glass, but shovelling the rubble kept me warm enough. It was only when I sat down by Sam Morris to split a stone that I really felt the pinch. I pulled my cap right down over my ears and rubbed my hands hard on my thighs to get the blood flowing before picking up the chisel.

As I tapped away with my hammer I could see Will Frongoch's feet and the shaking of the rope that kept him upright. Will was up on the rock face drilling a hole for the powder. By the time he was ready and shouting "Fire!" I was done with my stone, and had stacked my eleven slates. I followed Sam Morris to the fire shelter, and squeezed in between him and Tom's dad, who was spouting some poetry for the eisteddfod we were going to hold in the cabin midday. Before he'd finished spouting, the powder exploded. I felt the tremor rise from the ground and travel up my body. Sometimes I think the whole shed will rise in the air

and float away with us all in it. But the tremor stopped, the shed was steady, and we all spilled out again.

As soon as I got out, who should I see walking up but George Watson. He came plodding towards us with his thumb in his waistcoat pocket.

I looked away, so as not to catch his eye. I didn't want it to be me he was after. And especially not my Sparrowhawk. The other men had grown quiet too. They were just watching and waiting to hear what the steward had to say.

The air was still.

The only sound to be heard was the scrinch, scrinch, scrinch beneath the man's boots.

And then…

I felt a quiver.

A vibration in the air.

A sharpness that travelled through my bones.

In a split second I was hurling myself at Mr Watson and…

"And…" I swallowed hard and stared at the doctor with my heart beating fit to burst.

"And what?" he asked, gripping my shoulder.

"I think I pushed him to the ground," I said shakily. "I…Ah!" The 'Ah!' was a cry of shock as the doctor wrenched my shoulder back into place.

As the waves of pain ebbed away, I heard a voice say: "Steady there!" and nearly cried from shock again.

A man was standing in the doorway, a stocky jowly

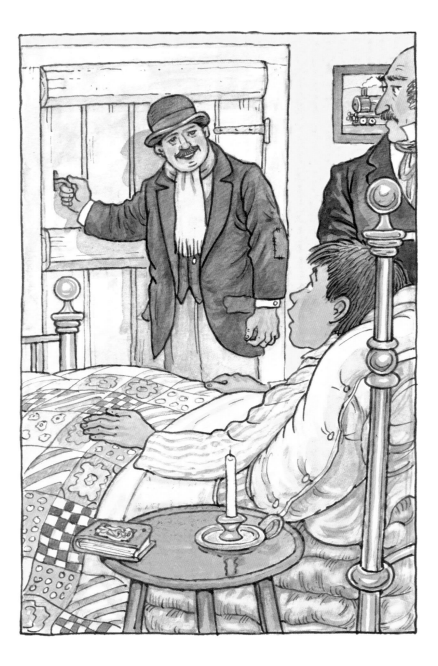

man with a gash on his forehead and a bruise that covered the whole of his left cheek.

"Mr Watson!" I gasped. "I... I didn't mean to!"

"Didn't you?" A strange look crossed the steward's face.

"Jack's hit his head and doesn't remember what exactly he did," the doctor said.

Mr Watson winced, though it may have been a smile.

Then he said in a stiff voice: "That whisper you heard up at the quarry, young Jack, that was the noise of a rock dislodging itself from high up on the cliff face. You know how it is. Sometimes, after a blast, the rocks higher up get destabilised. If you hadn't moved as fast as you did and pushed me out of the way, I'd have been caught under it and most likely killed. Brave man." He held out his hand.

I didn't take it. Not out of rudeness, but out of surprise.

George Watson nodded and made for the door again.

I waited.

Any moment now he's going to turn round, I thought. It'll be like that day when Mam fell. He was nice as pie till we got up to the top of the incline, then he sent me home. I cursed myself for gabbling out loud to the doctor about the Sparrowhawk.

Just then George Watson turned round.

"About that wild-car of yours, Jack Edwards."

"Yes, sir," I replied, and my face fell.

"I'll ask Lloyd the blacksmith to put a brake on for you. No use losing a good worker," he said smiling at me. "Especially one as fast as you."

I returned the smile.

"No, sir," I said.